Family Fiction

Writing Historical Fiction from your Family Tree

Jennifer Johnson Garrity

with Homeschool Tips and Schedule by Andrea Newitt

 BRIMWOOD PRESS

Copyright © 2006 by Brimwood Press
1941 Larsen Drive
Camino, CA 95709

All rights reserved

Special permission is granted exclusively to parent educators to reproduce workbook pages for use by immediate family members. No other part of this book may be reproduced or transmitted in any form without written permission from the publisher.

Cover Art: A Family Tree by Norman Rockwell
Printed by Permission of the Norman Rockwell Agency
Copyright © 1959 the Norman Rockwell Agency

Photographs: All photographs marked VGC are from the Vanishing Georgia Collection, courtesy of the Georgia Dept. of Archives and History.
All other photographs belong to the family archives of the author or publisher.

Graphic Design: Carmen Pereira Pucilowski

Manufactured in the United States of America
ISBN 978-0-9770704-1-1

Acknowledgements

Many thanks to Andrea Newitt for sharing her homeschooling expertise. Her donation of time and hard work have helped to make this writing guide all that it should be. Special thanks also to Kim Kautzer for her invaluable advice and skillful editing, and to Janie Till for acting as last-minute grammar consultant. I appreciate the many dedicated hours put in by graphic designer Carmen Pucilowski and the patient computer help given to me by my husband, Kim Garrity. And to my publisher Marcia Brim: thank-you for encouraging me to pursue this project. Without your persistence, it may never have happened.

Publisher's Note

We at BrimWood Press are pleased to introduce this new writing guide that not only exposes young writers to the process of creating historical fiction, but addresses one of their greatest challenges: inspiration. The author of this guide, Jennifer Johnson Garrity, has had two books published as a result of using the approach she outlines here. We believe her shared expertise will benefit the homeschooling community by enriching its writing assignments.

Additionally, we have asked Andrea Newitt, an experienced homeschooler, to provide a suggested schedule, tips and grading guidelines for use with younger students (ages 10-13.) It is our hope that she will be for you one of those respected friends you might call for advice in implementing a new product. Her suggestions and guidelines are an added value to an already rich product. High school students and younger experienced or naturally gifted writers should find the materials in Mrs. Garrity's guide sufficient.

Contents

Student Guide 1

Introduction 1
A Story Doesn't Appear Out of Nowhere

General Research 5
Interview – Phase One
Family Fiction Chart
Interview – Phase Two
Interview Questions

Specific Research 13
Choose Your Branch
Blending Fact and Fiction
Make Your Best Guess
Anachronism
Historical Photographs
Historical Research Notes

Writing Your Story 35
The Plot
Fact or Fiction?
Write a Story, Not a Report
Creating a Roadmap
Beginnings

Editing Your Story 45
Adjectives
Adverbs
Passive Language
Sentence Starters
Completing the Project
Student Checklist

Instructor's Notes 53

Answer Key 56
Instructor's Checklist

Andrea's Homeschool Tips 63
An Introduction
Schedule for Younger Students
Grading Guide

Family Tree

Student Guide

Introduction

The Most Common Lament

"Students, your assignment is to write a five page work of historical fiction."

A collective groan fills the classroom.

"But Teacher," whines a girl in the back row, "I can't do the assignment. I don't know what to write about!"

"None of us knows what to write about!" echo her classmates.

"Just use your imaginations," the teacher replies.

The young victims sigh and complain as they file out into the hallway. Set adrift in a sea of blank notebook pages, they flounder, desperate for something to keep them afloat. Most grasp at anything, hanging on long enough to create a lukewarm, uninspired story. Submitted in the nick of time, it succeeds in staving off academic failure. But before long it lies crumpled in the trashcan, forgotten by writer and reader alike.

FUL-352, Ca.1885 VGC

It doesn't have to be this way, for every student has a built-in treasure trove of inspiration for historical fiction: ancestors. In fact, the supply deepens and widens the farther back in history one reaches. There is enough fruit on each young writer's family tree to feed multiple works of fiction, if only he or she will take the time to harvest it. A story based on the life of an ancestor not only has personal relevance, it fosters close family relationships because of the communication necessary to begin the research process. It produces a quality of work that the average writing assignment fails to inspire, and instead of ending up in the trashcan, it becomes an heirloom.

> *"…every student has a built-in treasure trove of inspiration for historical fiction: ancestors."*

A Story Doesn't Appear Out Of Nowhere

Where do authors get their ideas? Do they appear out of thin air when the author sits down in front of a blank page? Or does something act as a spark to ignite the author's imagination?

YOUR TURN

List eight things that might spark an author's imagination, producing an idea for a story. Compare them with the list in the *Instructor's Notes* when you've finished.

1. _____   5. _____

2. _____   6. _____

3. _____   7. _____

4. _____   8. _____

Using a dictionary, define the following words. If the word has more than one meaning, which meaning do you think applies best to this assignment? Write it down. Check your definitions with those in the *Instructor's Notes*.

historical:

fiction:

Now combine both definitions to create a definition for:

historical fiction:

ancestor: (Latin) antecessor: "one that goes before"

One from whom a person is descended and who is usually more remote in the line of descent than a grandparent.

In other words, your ancestors are your great grandparents, your great-great grandparents, your great-great-great grandparents, and so on, all the way back to the beginning of time. For this project, however, you can include grandparents, and great aunts or uncles from whom you are not directly descended.

If you are adopted and don't have an opportunity to gather information about your birth ancestors, you may write about your adopted ancestors.

MY STORY

Before I was an author, I enjoyed the hobby of genealogical research. In other words, I spent my free time looking up information about my ancestors. I was curious about these people who came before me. What were their names? Where did they live and what was happening in the world during their lifetimes?

I knew my grandmother had been born in Missouri, and I knew the name of the town in which she was born. Armed with that little bit of information, I set to work looking for more. Gradually I learned the names and birthplaces of my great-grandparents, when they were married, where they lived...and I learned the same things about their parents. But these facts alone didn't satisfy my curiosity.

I began to wonder what their everyday lives were like. What did they talk about? How did they dress and what did they eat? What were they afraid of? What did they do for enjoyment? Unfortunately, my grandparents were no longer living, and my parents didn't know the answers to most of my questions.

So I decided to do some research. I began to read about Missouri. The more I read, the more I was able to fit together the pieces of my ancestors' lives. The Civil War caught my attention, because Missouri was a terrible place to be during that war. As I learned more about the fighting that separated families and destroyed friendships, I thought, "Someone should write a story about this!"

And then it occurred to me: *I'm* the one who's interested, so I should write the story. That's when I set to work writing *The Bushwhacker* (1999; Peachtree Publishers, Ltd.), a novel about Jacob and Eliza Knight and their struggle to survive in Civil War Missouri.

BOOK LIST

The following novels are just some of the many that are closely or loosely based on their authors' own family histories. Have you read any of them?

Tales From the Homeplace
Harriet Burandt, Shelley Dale
1997 Bantam/Doubleday/Dell

Gib Rides Home
Zilpha Keatley Snyder,
1998 Delacorte Press

Caddie Woodlawn, Magical Melons
Carol Ryrie Brink
1935, 1939 Macmillan

Sarah, Plain and Tall, Skylark
Patricia MacLachlan
1985, 1994 HarperCollins

Willow Wind Farm,
Stairstep Farm,
First Farm in the Valley,
Winding Valley Farm
Anne Pellowski
1981, 1982 Philomel Books

The Wolfling
Sterling North
1969 Scholastic, Inc.

Roll of Thunder,
Hear My Cry
Mildred D. Taylor
1976 Dial Books – 1991
Penguin Books USA Inc.

Little Britches: Father and I were Ranchers
Ralph Moody
1950 Ralph Moody –
1991 Bison Books

Imagine

You are sitting alone at a desk, pen in hand. You've been told to write a short, historical fiction story, but your mind is blank. "What do I write about?" you agonize.

Silent and unseen, your ancestors emerge from the shadows and gather around you. "Write about me," whispers Great-Great-Great-Great Grandpa Thomas, who led a cavalry charge in South Carolina during the Civil War.

"No, tell my story," pleads Great-Great Aunt Priscilla, born on a homestead in Montana. "I taught school in a one room schoolhouse and survived three days in a blizzard!"

"Choose me!" demands Great-Great Grandpa Ned, who bandaged wounded soldiers during the First World War.

Suddenly you have more choices than you know what to do with! You could pick any one of them, because each ancestor has a fascinating story to tell. It doesn't matter if they were rich or poor, famous or ordinary...they all lived interesting lives, because they lived through interesting times.

YOUR TURN

fact:

    a) a thing done

    b) the quality of being actual (real)

    In fact = In truth

Perhaps your parents or grandparents have shared some family history with you. Write down any interesting facts you already happen to know about your ancestors.

_____

_____

_____

_____

If you don't know anything about your ancestors, how could you find out?

_____

_____

General Research

Climbing Your Family Tree

Ever climb a tree? It's hard work. It takes effort to find secure footing and pull yourself upward from branch to branch. Climbing your family tree will take some effort too.

Interview – Phase One

The way to begin your climb is to INTERVIEW your parents, grandparents, and perhaps a few great aunts and uncles. The important thing is to find someone who knows about the family history.

You can interview family members in person, by telephone, via email or traditional mail. If interviewing by traditional mail, you might mail a copy of the chart on the following page to someone who can fill it out for you. Mail it together with Part Two of the interview phase (see following section).

Start your interview by filling out as much of the family tree chart on the following page as you can. You will find instructions on the chart. During this first part of the interview, all you need to ask are the basics: names, birth and death dates, birth and death places, and who married whom.

How far back can you go? My husband can list some of his ancestors all the way back to the 1400s in England. I can list mine only back to the 1700s. It doesn't matter; even if your family tree grows only 75 years high, it's still a tree and you can still climb it.

Family Fiction Chart

Start by making photocopies of the blank chart. Then write your own name, birth date, and birthplace at the "starting position." Next fill in your parents' information on the attached branches. Next fill in your grandparents' information, your great-grandparents', and so on. If your family has a large amount of genealogical information, place your grandparents in the "starting position" on one of your photocopies and proceed. You may need to fill out more than one chart as you follow a certain family line back in time. Once content with your photocopies and research transfer the most important information to your book and file the copies.

STARTING POSITION

Mother's Branch

Father's Branch

Interview – Phase Two

Now that you've filled out the chart with the basic facts, you're ready to climb a little higher. Your new goal is to find out as much extra information as you can about your ancestors.

Again, you will want to interview parents, grandparents, great-grandparents or other family members. Your job as interviewer is to bring forth all the interesting facts and anecdotes* they know about your family history. Chances are they won't be able to satisfy all your curiosity, but you'll be surprised at the fascinating things you discover simply by learning to ask the right kinds of questions.

YOUR TURN

Make a list of six specific questions to ask about your ancestors. Questions such as "What were my ancestors' lives like?", "What did my ancestors do?" and "How did my ancestors live?" are too general.

Here's a hint: think about what kinds of things interest you. Do you enjoy sports, pets, reading, travel, drawing or painting? Are you interested in clothing styles, games, jewelry, or cars? Ask questions about these specific types of things, such as: "Were any of our ancestors artists?" or "Did anyone in our family tree own a special pet?"

1. _____

2. _____

3. _____

4. _____

5. _____

6. _____

*anecdote: a short account of an interesting or humorous incident.

Interview Questions

Compare your questions to the list below. Did you already ask any of the following? If not, consider adding some or all of the questions below to your interview list. If you think of more, please add them.

1. From which country and why did our ancestors emigrate to this country?
2. Are there any funny stories about any of our ancestors?
3. Did anyone in our family tree accomplish something unique or special?
4. Did any of our ancestors invent anything?
5. Did anyone travel to an interesting place?
6. Did any ancestor of ours have peculiar character traits?
7. Did any ancestor of ours have a strange personality?
8. Did anything sad or tragic happen to any of our ancestors?
9. Did anyone die in an epidemic, or of a rare disease?
10. Was anyone in our family history involved in a war, either as soldier, medic, protestor?
11. Was one of our ancestors involved in a natural disaster, like a flood, fire or earthquake?
12. How about an accident, like a ship sinking or a train wreck?
13. Has a specific heirloom been handed down in our family? Perhaps a piece of furniture, jewelry, a watch, clock, or toy? What is the story behind it?
14. Was anyone involved in politics – campaigning for or holding public office, protesting something he or she didn't agree with, or joining in political movements such as women's suffrage, etc?
15. Are there any unsolved mysteries in our family history?

INTERVIEW NOTES: Space has been provided for you to write your questions and your family's response. The more questions you ask, the more useful information you're going to get.

REMEMBER: Photocopy the blank pages before you begin. You may receive more information than will fit into the space provided.

Interview Questionnaire

Question: _____
_____

Response: _____
_____
_____
_____

Question: _____
_____

Response: _____
_____
_____
_____

Question: _____
_____

Response: _____
_____
_____
_____

Question: _____
_____

Response: _____
_____
_____

Interview Date:
_____

Family Member Interviewed:
_____

_____

Interviewed by:
_____

Family Tree

Interview Date:

_____

Family Member Interviewed:

_____

_____

Interviewed by:

_____

Interview Questionnaire

Question: _____

_____

Response: _____

_____

_____

_____

Question: _____

_____

Response: _____

_____

_____

_____

Question: _____

_____

Response: _____

_____

_____

_____

Question: _____

_____

Response: _____

_____

_____

Interview Questionnaire

Question: _____

_____

Response: _____

_____

_____

_____

Question: _____

_____

Response: _____

_____

_____

_____

Question: _____

_____

Response: _____

_____

_____

_____

Question: _____

_____

Response: _____

_____

_____

Interview Date:

_____

Family Member Interviewed:

_____

_____

Interviewed by:

_____

Family Tree

Interview Date:

_____

Family Member Interviewed:

_____

_____

Interviewed by:

_____

Interview Questionnaire

Question: _____
_____

Response: _____
_____
_____
_____

Question: _____
_____

Response: _____
_____
_____
_____

Question: _____
_____

Response: _____
_____
_____
_____

Question: _____
_____

Response: _____
_____
_____

Specific Research

Choose Your Branch

When you climb a tree, you eventually have to make a choice about which direction to go. Several branches may be strong enough to hold you, but you can only sit on one of them at a time. It's the same with your family tree.

Let's say you find out that your great-great-great grandfather, Jack, fought in France during World War One. You also find out that a distant ancestor, whose name you aren't sure of, was born into the Lakota Sioux tribe AND that Mollie, another distant ancestor, traveled the Oregon Trail back in 1849. All three would make an exciting story...but you need to decide between them. You can only write one story at a time. Which one of the three will you base this assignment on?

The best way to make the decision is to ask yourself: whose life is most interesting to me, the author? If you're more interested in Native American history than the Oregon Trail or World War One, then by all means, write about your Native American ancestor. If you happen to find Mollie's life on the Oregon Trail fascinating, then base your story on her experiences. If the Great War intrigues you, then it makes sense to base your story on Great-Great Grandpa Jack.

If you have a personal interest in a subject, you're going to enjoy writing about it. If an author enjoys writing a story, his reader will catch his enthusiasm and have a great time reading it.

YOUR TURN

Write down the name of the ancestor you've decided to base your story on. Beneath his or her name, list the reasons you chose this particular person.

_____

_____

_____

_____

_____

_____

"Whose life is most interesting to me?"

What does it Mean to "Base a Story" on Someone?

A base is a foundation. If a story is based on a real person, that person's life is the foundation of the story. You start with the basic facts about that person, and build upward, adding layers of fiction.

Your story can be **closely** or **loosely** based on an ancestor.

If you know a great amount of detail about your chosen ancestor, then your story will be closely based on his life. Maybe you know exactly where he lived, what he did for a living, and perhaps even things he said or thought are recorded in a diary your family owns.

If you know only a few facts about your chosen ancestor, your story will be loosely based on her life. You will have to use your imagination to fill in the gaps.

Whether your story is closely or loosely based on an ancestor, you will need to build upward on the foundation of his or her life.

How is it done? … by …

Blending Fact and Fiction

Remember:

fiction is:

    a) something invented by the imagination

    b) an invented story

fact is:

    a) a thing done

    b) the quality of being real, or true

Make Your Best Guess

Without doing any research, try answering the following questions:

How did farmers harvest wheat in the early 1800s?

How did a woman on the Oregon Trail wash her family's clothing?

How would you set a table for dinner in a farmhouse in colonial America? (1700s)

How did people travel from place to place during the Middle Ages in Europe?

Compare your answers with those in the *Instructor's Notes*. Probably you know some of the above answers; most likely you only know part of the information.

My novel, *The Bushwhacker*, contains certain facts:

1. The places my ancestors lived in Missouri
2. The jobs some of them held (storekeeper and sheriff)
3. Some of my ancestors' names
4. Missouri's climate, plant life, animals, and landscape
5. The Civil War and the names and places of certain battles
6. Details about how people dressed, ate, talked, worked and traveled 150 years ago.

MY TURN

When I wrote *The Bushwhacker*, based on my family tree, I uncovered many historical facts to include in my novel. My aunt was able to tell me where my ancestors had lived in Missouri, but I needed to look at census records to find out what kinds of jobs they held. I also discovered many of their names on the census records. Because I grew up on the West Coast and wasn't familiar with Missouri, I used an encyclopedia to learn about its climate, plant life, landscape and animals. I also looked in books about birds, animals, and plants to see which ones were common in Missouri. History books and documentaries helped me learn about the Civil War, and the Internet, history books, and historical novels were an excellent source of knowledge about how people lived daily life 150 years ago.

FLO-151, Confederate Soldiers, ca. 1863 VGC

YOUR TURN

Using a dictionary, define:

census:

Compare your definition with the definition in the *Instructor's Section*.

The United States National Archives have census records dating back to 1790. The census takers visited each farm, house and apartment, asking people questions and writing down their answers. The pages they wrote on have been preserved, and are available for us to look at today! They contain all kinds of useful information, such as people's exact addresses, where they and their parents were born, what languages they spoke, what kind of jobs they held, their children's names, etc.

Many census records are available on the Internet. Try visiting www.census-online.com or www.censusfinder.com.

OR, if you're lucky enough to live near one of the Federal archives in the United States, you can visit and take a look at the census records there. The Instructor's Section has a complete listing of Federal archives.

Most archives have military records as well. Many genealogy websites can help you access them. By looking through these records, you may be able to find out if any of your ancestors served in the military, participated in any wars, and if so, where and for how long.

Which Research Tools Would You Use?

What kinds of tools would you use to discover the above details about the places your ancestors lived?

_____

_____

_____

_____

What kinds of tools would one use to learn about the Civil War or other famous historical events?

_____

_____

_____

_____

Where would you look to find details about how people dressed, talked, ate, traveled, worked, etc. during a certain period in history?

_____

_____

_____

_____

Compare your answers to those in the *Instructor's Section*.

As an author of historical fiction, it is your job to become knowledgeable about the time period in which your story takes place. You must do enough research to avoid *anachronism*.

Anachronism

Using a dictionary, define:

anachronism:

chronology:

IMAGINE...settling down to read an adventure novel about a slave girl in 1858 who escapes from her master and makes her way north to freedom. Your heart beats faster as you read; you feel like you're right there with her as she rumbles, concealed beneath a pile of straw in a farm wagon, toward a "safe house." A woman hurries out to greet the wagon and usher the girl inside where she will prepare her a...frozen microwave dinner? Later, the girl will hide in the woman's attic, watching...television?

Suddenly the mood is broken – you aren't in the slave girl's world anymore, and you can't trust the author of that book to lead you into a historical time period.

Frozen dinners, microwaves and television don't belong in the year 1858. **Anachronism**, then, is a failure to place a person, event, object, or custom in its proper time period.

YOUR TURN

List five examples of anachronism. (such as: a knight in armor driving a truck on the freeway)

1. _____

2. _____

3. _____

4. _____

5. _____

NOTE: Speech can be anachronistic. Two hundred and fifty years ago, people didn't say, "That's cool!" or "Let's hang out together after school."

When you've chosen your story's time period, see if you can find some common expressions from that era by reading books or websites about daily life during that time period. Use a few of them in your story to make it more authentic.

Names can be anachronistic too. Most likely you'll know your actual ancestors' names, but what about adding extra, fictional characters to your story? Beware of using the wrong names in certain time periods! For example, girls generally weren't named Chelsea or Madison and boys weren't named Trey or Ryan back in 1850. If you're having trouble finding appropriate names:

1. Take a good look at your or another person's family tree to see which names were used during certain time periods.

2. Look up a news article or history website about your era. Look for names.

3. The Bible is a good source of names for historical fiction. People have been using Bible names for their children for many hundreds of years.

Are You A Trustworthy Guide?

You, as the author of historical fiction, must be a trustworthy guide as you lead your reader into another time period. The reader is counting on you to lead her into an accurate historical setting so she can experience the story as if she were right there in the middle of it.

YOUR TURN

Using a dictionary, define:

accurate:

How can you provide an accurate setting? By doing research and including accurate, interesting facts about your time period.

MY TURN

My novel, *The Bushwhacker*, started small, then grew as I did research and discovered interesting facts about life in the 1860s. Facts such as:

- Succotash: A stew of corn and beans commonly eaten in Missouri

- Bushwhackers: Men who fought on the side of the South in Civil War era Missouri, without actually joining the Confederate Army.

- Skull pegging: Back in the 1820s, when someone was scalped during battle with Native American tribes, a doctor used to drill holes in his skull to help it heal. Henry, a character in *The Bushwhacker*, explains how this happened to him in his youth.

I added that last detail, along with the two previous ones, because I knew it would make my book more interesting to the reader.

The HISTORICAL RESEARCH PAGES included in this workbook are for you to store all the fascinating facts you discover about the setting and time period of your story. Are you prepared to use the right tools? Try to take notes while using as many as possible of the following:

    Encyclopedia

    Television documentaries

    Books on plant life

    History book (about setting)

    Books on wildlife

    Historical movies

    Books with photos of your setting

    Paintings

    Websites with any of the above

    Old family photographs

    Census records

    Military records

    Topographical map

    A history teacher/expert (such as a museum docent)

Historical Photographs

Using Photographs For Research

Many families possess photographs of ancestors. These photos can be a valuable source of information! Observe them carefully and try to discover what your ancestors looked like, what kinds of houses they lived in, how they dressed, and many other details about their daily lives.

Is there a house, car or horse-drawn wagon in the background? How about a family pet? What objects do you see around the people in the photo? What details can you notice about the hairstyles, jewelry, or clothing in the photo?

If you have chosen to write about an ancestor who lived before cameras were invented, then find a book or website showing paintings from your chosen time period. Such paintings can also be a valuable source of information.

YOUR TURN

Study each of the following photographs and write down your observations underneath or in the margins. What historical details do you observe? How do the people's clothing, hairstyles, tools and surroundings differ from today?

EMN-5, Grandmother and Child, ca.1900 VGC

Note: the child in this photograph is a boy. How do his clothing and bicycle differ from those of today?

_____
_____
_____
_____
_____
_____
_____

CAR-171, Coca-Cola Delivery, ca. 1904 VGC

How do soft drinks arrive at your local grocery store?

_____
_____
_____
_____
_____
_____
_____
_____

Did your baby stroller look like this?

Why wouldn't this stroller be convenient today?

LAU-56, Baby in Wicker Carriage, ca.1890 VGC

How does this compare to a modern harvest?

DEK-2, Harvesting Wheat, ca. 1910 VGC

Notice the coal-burning stove in the middle of the room. Why do you think the desks are arranged like this?

RAN-207, One Room School, ca. 1900 VGC

RAB-136, Cooking Class, 1905 VGC

What equipment might you see in a modern-day cooking class?

Would someone working with fire today wear protective gear?

What kind?

MOR-029-001, Blacksmith, date unknown VGC

What do you wear when you go swimming?

HAL-178, Ready to Swim, ca. 1911 VGC

How do these football uniforms compare to those worn today?

CLR-146, Football Team, ca. 1898 VGC

Notice the office equipment. Could a modern office run smoothly with what you see here?

MUS-152, Real Estate and Insurance Office, 1897 VGC

What kinds of chores do you do around home?

GWN-83, Picking Cotton VGC

How would this change your telephone conversations?

GWN-239 First Telephone in Town VGC

What might happen if this automobile had an accident?

WTF-231, 1903 Oldsmobile VGC

Does the boy next door to you dress like this?

Chicago, ca. 1913

Historical Research Notes

Fill out the following pages. Remember, you are concerned only with your story's setting and the years during which your story takes place. You don't need to record what was going on in the rest of the world or in other time periods, unless it has a direct connection with your story.

Not all of the following sections will pertain to your story. Concentrate on the ones that do, but remember that the more historical information you discover, the more you have to work with when writing your story. The more interesting historical details you include, the richer your story will be.

My Story Takes Place in (State or Province, Town, County, River, Mountain Range, etc.): _____

During the Year(s): _____

Landscape: _____

Wildlife: _____

Climate: _____

Plant Life (Trees, Grasses, Herbs, Flowers, Bushes): _____

HISTORICAL EVENTS

Wars: _____

Natural Disasters: _____

_____

_____

_____

Political Changes (Such as Elections): _____

_____

_____

_____

Famous People: _____

_____

_____

_____

EVERYDAY LIFE:

Food: _____

_____

_____

Clothing and Shoes:

   Men: _____

   _____

   _____

   Women: _____

   _____

   _____

   Children: _____

Military Uniforms: _____

_____

_____

Transportation: _____

_____

_____

Housing: _____

_____

_____

_____

Hairstyles:

    Men: _____

    _____

    Women: _____

    _____

    Children: _____

    _____

Commonly Used First Names: _____

_____

_____

Common (Speech) Expressions: _____

_____

_____

_____

Common Jobs or Chores:

Men: _____

_____

_____

Women: _____

_____

_____

Children: _____

_____

Weapons: _____

_____

Tools: _____

_____

_____

Toys: _____

_____

Machinery: _____

_____

_____

Schooling: _____

_____

_____

_____

_____

Details Noted from your Family Photographs:

More Notes:

Writing Your Story

YOUR TURN

Using a dictionary, define:

plot:

Compare your definition with the one in the *Instructor's Notes*.

The Plot

Have you ever looked closely at a piece of woven cloth or tapestry? You'll see various colored weft threads woven through the warp threads. Before a weaver can create a piece of cloth, she sets the warp threads, which run lengthwise along the loom. Then she weaves the weft (sideways) threads into the warp threads to create a unique design.

Your job as a writer of historical fiction is to weave together fact and fiction, just as I did when writing *The Bushwhacker*. I knew my ancestors lived in Missouri during the 1860s. I knew what town they lived in, and what some of their jobs were. Those facts were my warp threads, already set on the loom. When I added fiction to those facts, the combination created an exciting story, just as a beautiful pattern is formed when brightly colored weft threads are woven into the warp. I had no proof that one of my ancestors was actually a bushwhacker, but after learning about bushwhackers in my research, I decided to add one to my story in order to give it an exciting plot.

Picture yourself as a weaver, sitting down to your loom. As you weave your story, you will blend fact and fiction into a unique design. But there are some rules to follow. In historical fiction, certain parts of the story must be fact and certain parts must be fiction.

How do you come up with a plot? By weaving together fact and fiction.

Fact or Fiction?

Can some parts of the story be both fact AND fiction? The following list will give you a guideline to follow. Think of these eleven story elements as "threads" in your tapestry.

Larger Place Names must be FACT.

If your novel takes place in New England, you will need to use the name of an actual state and/or town.

Smaller Place Names can be FACT or FICTION.

It is okay to create a fictional place name for a smaller location, such as a village or farm.

Characters' Names can be FACT or FICTION.

You could use your ancestors' real names, or you might choose to change their names slightly. For example, in The Bushwhacker, I changed my ancestors' last name from Canada to Canaday because I thought readers might be distracted by a last name that was the same as a country. Since the country Canada had nothing to do with my story, I added the "y" in order to keep the name as close as possible to the real thing, yet change it enough to correct the problem. The story can still be based on your ancestors, whether or not you choose to use their exact names.

Characters' Appearance can be FACT or FICTION.

If you know your great-great grandmother had red hair and freckles, then go ahead and describe her that way in your story. But if all you have is an old black and white or sepia photograph, or no photograph at all, then give her the hair color and appearance of your choice. Or use what features you can see in a photograph, and make up the rest. Another option is to take a good look at yourself and other family members who are directly descended from the ancestor you have chosen to write about. If none of you have brown eyes, then chances are good your ancestor didn't either. You may even want to choose a living relative and base your physical description of the ancestor in your story on that person's own features and coloring.

Famous Events Such as Wars, Battles, Political Elections, and Natural Disasters must be FACT.

Not only does a reader want to be entertained by historical fiction, he wants to learn something about that time period, too. The historical events that surround your characters must be accurate.

Dates and Times of Famous Events (Such as Above) must be FACT.

If the great San Francisco earthquake of 1906 took place in April in the early morning hours, then you don't want to say it happened on an October evening. Take time to research the exact times and seasons of any famous events you include in your story. Accuracy in this area will help your reader feel like she is really experiencing an event the way it happened.

Dialogue (Conversations Between Your Characters) must be FICTION.

Since you weren't present with a tape recorder 200 years ago, you have no way of knowing just what your ancestor William said to his brother Benjamin as they prepared to go off and fight in the war of 1812. You will need to imagine what they might have said to each other.

Characters' Thoughts and Feelings must be FICTION.

Once again, you weren't there for great-great grandma Isabel to tell you her thoughts about the great flu epidemic of 1918. You, the author, will have to supply her thoughts out of your own imagination. (The only exception to this rule is if your family is fortunate enough to possess an heirloom diary or journal in which your ancestor recorded her exact thoughts and feelings in detail. If you have a treasure like this, then by all means, use it!)

Characters' Actions can be FACT or FICTION.

This depends on how much information you have about the ancestor you've chosen to write about. For instance, you may know for sure that your great grandfather won first prize in a calf-roping contest in 1938, and that he took a canoe trip down the Colorado River later that same year. Most likely you will want to use these factual events in your story. But maybe, to make the story more exciting, you want to say that he rescued a drowning girl from the river. You are free to add this made-up action to the story, because it is fiction BASED on his life, not a report about his life. If you know a lot of detail about your great grandfather's actions and find them interesting enough on their own, then you may choose not to add anything.

Objects Surrounding Your Characters can be FACT or FICTION.

Objects must be factual in the sense that they are true to the time period in which your story takes place. If you're writing about a distant ancestor who sailed to America on the Mayflower, you will want to make sure that her clothing, eating utensils, and furniture are not anachronistic, but actually were in use during her lifetime.

Objects can be fictional in the sense that you may have no idea whether or not your distant ancestor owned a trunk made of cedar-wood, but you choose to give her one anyway, because it is part of your plot and you know that cedar wood trunks were in use during her lifetime.

And if your family possesses a certain heirloom handed down from the ancestor you are writing about, then go ahead and put it in your story.

Important or Famous People (Who Appear in Your Story) must be FACT.

Maybe you want to color your story by adding a real historical figure to it. Let's suppose that in your story, one of your ancestors in colonial Virginia is walking down a country lane one day, when young George Washington rides by on a horse. If young George's hair was black, you don't want to say it was blond. If he had light blue eyes, you don't want to call them "dark." Feel free to include famous people, and even allow them to speak a few words of fictional dialogue. But the way they speak, their appearance, and whereabouts must be historically accurate. (Your relative wouldn't encounter George Washington in New Mexico, would he?)

Also, if you mention the name of the President of the United States during a story that takes place in 1814, then be sure you know exactly who was President during that time, and the correct spelling of his name.

YOUR TURN

Use the above list to fill out the chart below. Place all eleven "threads" under their correct heading. For example, OBJECTS will go under the "can be EITHER" heading, because though an object's existence during your story's time period must be factual, the idea of your ancestor actually using or seeing that object might be fictional. You can refer to this chart as you write, in order to make sure you are using each "thread" correctly. After you fill it out, compare it to the chart on page 58 of the *Instructor's Notes*.

FACT	can be EITHER	FICTION
1. _____	1. _____	1. _____
2. _____	2. _____	2. _____
3. _____	3. _____	
4. _____	4. _____	
	5. _____	

Write A Story, Not A Report

Remember – you are writing a story, not a factual report on how people lived during a certain historical time period. You want your reader, first of all, to enjoy the story. Secondly, you want him to learn a little about its historical setting as he reads. Just as you wouldn't dump a mound of salt onto a plate of food, you don't want to dump a mound of historical information into one paragraph and serve it to your reader. You sprinkle salt lightly over your food, and you want to sprinkle factual information lightly throughout the story.

For instance, suppose you learn in your research that girls used to wear pantalettes (long, frilly, undergarments) back in the 1820s. They also used parasols to keep the sun off their heads, wore kidskin gloves and sausage curls in their hair. You could tell your reader all that information by interrupting the story and dumping it on him all at once, like this:

> *Annette wore her hair in sausage curls. She had a parasol that she always carried with her to keep the sun off her head, and she wore pantalettes every day. She also wore a pair of kid gloves.*

But if you do, the reader will feel like he's reading a report on how women dressed in the 1820s. He might feel frustrated and bored, because what he really wants is to find out what's going to happen next.

It's much better to sprinkle historical facts throughout the story so they become a natural part of the action:

> *Annette finished arranging her hair in sausage curls, then looked out the window to see if her carriage had arrived.*
>
> *"He's here!" she called to her sister when she saw the driver and his team of horses waiting near the front door. She grabbed her parasol and kidskin gloves and hurried downstairs. As she dashed out the door, her pantalettes caught on one of the hinges, jerking her to a stop.*
>
> *At the loud, ripping sound, the driver glanced up.*
>
> *Embarrassed, Annette unhooked her torn pantalettes and climbed into the carriage.*

You've added a few historical facts here and there while continuing to tell your story. This way, the reader learns about life in the 1820s without having to be interrupted as he enjoys the story's action.

A Mound of Salt, or a Sprinkling of Salt

Now it's Time to Create a Roadmap

A driver doesn't set off on a trip without having some idea of where he's going, though he may not know in advance every turn he is going to make and every side road down which he'll travel. Just like that driver, you need to have a general idea of where your story is headed. You will need to create a ROADMAP. Your roadmap will serve as a guide to help you keep your story on track.

However, as you write, new ideas will come to you, causing you to make changes in your "travel plans." You might say, "Hey, wait a minute! I could have my character stop and pan for gold as he takes that train trip through California!" That's perfectly fine. Just do a little adjusting of your roadmap, or toss the first one aside and write a whole new one. You could end up with as many as five to ten roadmaps as your ideas change throughout the writing process.

Your roadmap can also include notes to yourself, or questions that will need to be answered. You may not have decided on certain things yet, but that doesn't need to stop you from writing a roadmap. Just include your questions in parentheses, and make your decisions later, as you write the story.

Your roadmap can be as short as a paragraph, or as long as two pages, depending on how much detail you want to include in it. My advice is to keep it short, and save your writing energy for the actual story.

Here's an Example of a Basic Roadmap:

Anna Jones is tired of teaching school in the tiny schoolhouse in Montana. The winters are too cold for her. She longs for adventure. Anna and her friend Julia buy train tickets to sunny California. Neither of them has been there before, but they dream of eating an orange whenever they want, and marrying rich husbands. During the train trip, Anna begins to get homesick. (She misses her younger sister most...or maybe her twin brother?). In California, Anna and her friend have to work hard in the kitchen of a hotel (or as maids, cleaning the rooms?) just to earn enough money to survive. Julia gets married and moves away to Arizona. Now Anna is really alone. She decides that Montana isn't so bad after all, because her loved ones are there. When she finally makes the long trip home, her whole family and all of her former students are waiting for her at the train station.

NOTE: Beware of trying to include too many characters in a short story. (If you are an older student writing a novella or novel, then you can work more characters in).

YOUR TURN

The section below provides a place for you to create a roadmap. If you have trouble knowing where to start, ask yourself these questions: who, when, where, what, and why? As the answers come to you, write them down.

Roadmap

Beginnings

You are almost ready to begin writing your story. Before you start, take a look at the following list of possible ways to begin a story.

Description of a Person

Example: Jake Bryant had black hair and sparkling blue eyes. He was the shortest boy in his class, and everyone called him "Teeny."

Description of a Place

Example: The Mullins family homestead was flat and barren. The ground froze solid in the winter and dried into a hard crust in summer.

Dialogue

Example: "Wait for me, Cassie!" called Jonathan as he chased his older sister along the riverbank.

Cassie glanced behind her and kept running. "Catch up with me!"

Action

Example: Josiah Lane lifted his rifle and aimed at the grizzly bear. For one terrifying minute, the world fell silent. Then the grizzly leaped forward, swiping a huge claw at the hunter.

Description of Several Characters

Example: Linnea, Emilie, and Hattie sat together on the rag rug looking at a worn-out picture book. They had blond hair and ragged dresses, and Hattie's nose ran constantly. Emilie's hair had a reddish glow that made her sisters envious.

A Narrator who Remembers the Story

Maybe you want to have your ancestor tell his own story as if he is remembering it. In this case, be careful to write the whole story (and not just the beginning) from the narrator's perspective.

Example: One winter morning, Mother hurried into my bedroom and shook me awake. "Get up, Jimmy," she said. "The British Army is coming closer, and we have to get out of here."

Introduce a Character's Thoughts or Ideas

Example: Colonel John Jamison believed in hard work and a healthy diet. He always insisted his family eat three different kinds of vegetables with every meal.

YOUR TURN

Experiment with the above beginnings. Go back and write a beginning for your own story in the space below each example. Then decide which type of beginning is right for your story.

Now it's time to write the **rough draft** of your story. Remember, a rough draft doesn't have to be perfect.

1. Write your rough draft by hand on lined notebook paper so that you can cross things out, scribble corrections, or jot down notes to yourself in the margins.

2. When you've finished, stop and read over your rough draft, making sure your story makes sense and is historically accurate, containing no anachronisms.

3. Make sure you haven't tried to fit too many characters into a short story. If so, try to combine or eliminate some of them. If it's painful to discard a character you especially like, save him or her for another story.

4. Transfer your rough draft to the computer, using DOUBLE SPACING. This is a good time to make changes to your story, correcting historical or character problems, adding or subtracting dialogue, action, description, etc. Once you have printed out this first computer draft, you are ready to move on to the Editing Your Story section.

Editing Your Story

Using a dictionary, define the verb:

edit:

Compare it to the definition in the *Instructor's Notes*.

Your story is a diamond in the rough, which needs to be cut and polished in order to shine as a beautiful gem. This cutting and polishing is the editing process.

Prepare to edit your first computer draft, using a pen or pencil. The following four problems are some of the most common challenges young writers face.

Adjectives

What if your mom dressed up for a party and entered the room with fifteen bracelets on her arm, ten pair of earrings on her ears, lipstick all over her face and a dress covered with twenty different colors of sparkling sequins? Would you be embarrassed to be seen with her? Would you even be able to recognize her under all that "stuff"?

Think of your story in the same way. Piling on adjectives distracts from the natural beauty of your story. So, if you've got a...

> skinny, stringbeany, gaunt, scarecrow of a man

in your story, you'll need to decide which of the above adjectives (and they are all good ones!) best describes your character. Choose that one, and set the rest aside. Maybe you can use them in another part of the same story, or in a different story altogether.

YOUR TURN

Search your story for overuse of adjectives. Choose the best ones, and cut out the rest. Mark the changes on your printed first computer draft.

Watch for too many Adjectives

Watch for too many Adverbs

Adverbs

Adverbs do indeed help verbs, but only a weak verb needs to be helped. Do you want your story to be filled with weak verbs that limp along on crutches?

Now and then it's okay to use a weak verb like:

> move
> walk
> sat
> stood
> said
> look

… and attach an adverb to it in order to show the reader more clearly what is going on. For example:

> He **moved** quietly along.
> She **walked** crookedly.
> He **sat** tiredly in the chair.
> She **stood** up quickly.
> "Stop it!" she **said** angrily.
> The detective **looked** carefully at the evidence.

But what if you chose strong verbs instead of weak ones? What if you chose verbs that didn't need to lean on adverbs like a pair of crutches? Suppose you wrote:

> He **crept** along.
> She **staggered**.
> He **sank** into the chair.
> She **sprang** up.
> "Stop it!" she **snapped**.
> The detective **inspected** the evidence.

The above verbs don't need adverbs because they are strong and they do a fantastic job of **showing** the reader what is going on.

YOUR TURN

Inspect your first computer draft for weak verbs and change as many as you can to strong ones. Remember that it's okay now and then to use a weak one, especially "said." It's also okay to use adverbs now and then; just try not to use too many of them. Mark the changes so they can be clearly seen.

Passive Language

The key here is to watch for overuse of the words "was" and "were." Look at the following example:

Jill and Stephen were standing on Jill's front lawn. Suddenly Stephen looked up and saw that a red car was headed down the street. The driver was a young man with frizzy hair, and he was speeding wildly. His car was nearly spinning out of control. Jill was curious about him, so she took a closer look as he was driving past. When they saw the angry look on the driver's face, Jill and Stephen were scared.

Does that put you to sleep? It seems as if there's almost no action going on. Now check out the following paragraph:

Jill and Stephen were standing on Jill's front lawn. Suddenly Stephen looked up and saw a red car headed down the street. The driver, a young man with frizzy hair, sped wildly. His car nearly spun out of control. Curious, Jill took a closer look as he drove past. Seeing the angry look on his face, Jill and Steven felt scared.

Sounds better, doesn't it? With only one passive verb (were) and more direct action on the part of Jill, Stephen, and the driver, the paragraph moves quickly and keeps the reader's interest. Passive language not only slows down exciting action scenes, but it can slow down a simple narration as well. Consider the following example:

The Gonzales brothers were all very different from one another. Ernesto was the eldest, and he enjoyed school. He got good grades and was determined to become a doctor. The middle brother, Alfredo, was more happy-go-lucky. He didn't care that he was always flunking his classes. The youngest brother, José, was a mixture of both his older brothers. He knew how to study and how to play, and he was always able to decide when it was time to do either.

Compare that dull paragraph with the following:

The Gonzales brothers weren't anything alike. Ernesto, the eldest, enjoyed school. Determined to become a doctor, he got good grades. The middle brother, happy-go-lucky Alfredo, always flunked his classes. The youngest brother, José, was a mixture of both his older brothers. He knew how to study and how to play, and could always decide when it was time to do either.

Instead of eight passive verbs, we now have only three, and the Gonzales brothers seem much more alive and active.

YOUR TURN

Now check your first computer draft for passive language. If you find too many places where you've used the word "was" and "were" instead of direct action, cross some of them out and reword.

Watch for too much Passive Language

Use a Variety of Sentence Starters

Your story will read more smoothly if you resist the temptation to begin every sentence with a subject followed by a verb, such as:

Carl grabbed the hoe and lifted it high. The snake raised its head to strike. Carl jumped backward, bringing down the hoe with all his strength. The hoe missed its mark. Carl raised it again. He struck with angry force, desperate to kill the snake. The hoe hit the snake right on the head, killing it instantly. Carl returned to his grandfather's house, proudly carrying his conquered enemy.

Sounds monotonous, doesn't it? A good rule to follow is to try not to use the same type of sentence beginning more than twice in a row, so the paragraph reads more like this:

Carl grabbed the hoe and lifted it high. The snake raised its head to strike. Jumping backward, Carl brought down the hoe with all his strength. The hoe missed its mark. Carl raised it again. Desperate to kill the snake, he struck with angry force. The hoe hit the snake right on the head, killing it instantly. Proudly carrying his conquered enemy, Carl returned to his grandfather's house.

In the above paragraph, three subject-verb sentences have been replaced with other types of sentence starters, and the paragraph reads much more smoothly. Not having to read the same kind of sentence over and over again is a real relief to the reader!

Possibilities for sentence beginnings are:

Subject:

The train screeched and puffed away into the night.

George told Elizabeth he planned to leave town forever.

It was the fanciest birthday cake Setsuko had ever seen.

Preposition:

Beyond the stream, Cyrus found the perfect place to build a home.

In a terrible rush, Beulah scribbled a good-bye note and packed her suitcase.

Since he was eight years old, Benjamin had dreamed of flying a plane.

Adverb: (words ending in "ly")

Eagerly watching for her mother, Becky hummed her favorite song.

Foolishly ignoring the warning sign, Jack dove into shallow water.

Present Participle: (words ending in "ing") NOTE: The thing after the comma is the thing doing the "ing."

Gazing out the window, Maria frowned at the storm clouds.

Sitting on the dusty shelf, the ragged teddy bear seemed lost and lonely.

Past Participle:

Born and raised in a New York mansion, Bartholomew had grown accustomed to having servants.

Fooled by the thief's good manners, Angela allowed him to hold her purse while she tied her shoe.

Disappointed by her friend's broken promises, Martha determined never to trust her again.

Clausal: (when, while, where, since, as, if, although, because)

Although Thomas was angry, he held his tongue.

Since Amanda knew her mother was resting, she played quietly.

Because Harold feared heights, he refused to climb the tower.

If Martin had known danger awaited him in the woods, he would have kept to the path.

Adjective:

Delicate as a china teacup, Delia caught every cold that went around.

Aggressive and angry, Robert took on the role of neighborhood bully.

Suspicious, Catherine decided to investigate.

NOTE: The words "since", "before" and "after" can be used as both prepositional and clausal sentence openings.

YOUR TURN

Check your first computer draft for paragraphs in which you might have gotten into the rut of using one kind of sentence starter too many times in a row. See if you can reword some of these and begin them differently. Remember to follow the general rule of not using the same kind of sentence starter more than twice in a row. Mark changes clearly on your paper.

Completing the Project

Make all the above changes on the computer, then print out a second computer draft.

Now check your second computer draft for spelling errors, run-on or incomplete sentences, and punctuation problems. This is the time to add any additional last-minute dialogue, description, or historical facts you feel will strengthen your story. Mark these changes on your paper.

Make all the above changes on your computer and print out a third computer draft. Go over it one last time for typographical errors and other small problems that may have been missed.

It is always a good idea to have someone else take a good look at the story before printing out the final copy. As the writer, you may have looked at a misspelling or a grammatical or punctuation mistake so many times that you don't even notice it. Another proofreader will catch the mistakes you miss.

Once your story has been proofread, print out the final copy (THIS SHOULD BE SINGLE-SPACED). You may want to bind it in a cover you have decorated yourself, possibly including a photograph or drawing of the ancestor on whose life your story is based.

The last thing you do will be to put together a Family Fiction Binder. In this binder you will store the notes you took while conducting family interviews, the family tree chart (or charts) you filled out, your historical research notes, rough draft, and the final copy of your story

Congratulations!
You have created an heirloom
to be treasured by your family
for many years to come.

Student Checklist

Preparation:
- ___ Family Fiction chart filled out
- ___ Specific interview questions written
- ___ Interviews completed
- ___ Specific ancestor and story setting chosen
- ___ Family photographs, general historical photographs and/or paintings studied
- ___ Historical Research notes completed
- ___ Roadmap written
- ___ Type of story beginning chosen

Writing:
- ___ Rough draft hand-written
- ___ Rough draft checked for **content:**
  - ___ story reads as fiction and not as a "report"
  - ___ plot makes sense and flows well
  - ___ story weaves together fact and fiction (is believable and interesting)
  - ___ story contains enough historical facts to make the reader feel like he or she is "in" the time period and setting (for example: descriptions of clothing, food, travel, tools, chores, houses, etc.)
- ___ story is historically accurate
- ___ story contains no anachronisms
- ___ (short) story doesn't have too many characters
- ___ historical facts are "sprinkled throughout the story and not "dumped"
- ___ story's setting is clearly described (place names, landscape, climate, true historical events)
- ___ story includes dialogue
- ___ dialogue is appropriate to the story's time period and setting
- ___ Rough draft transferred to computer (double spaced) and printed out

Editing:

__ First computer draft checked for **style:**

  __ story has a strong title that creates interest

  __ story has a strong beginning that draws the reader in

  __ story does not have too many adjectives

  __ story contains strong verbs and not too many adverbs

  __ story does not have too much passive language

  __ story has a good variety of sentence starters

  __ story has a satisfying conclusion (reader is not left hanging)

  __ tense is consistent (the story doesn't jump back and forth between past and present tense)

__ Second computer draft checked for **mechanics:**

  __ spelling errors

  __ run-on sentences

  __ incomplete sentences

  __ punctuation errors

  __ typographical errors

__ Third computer draft checked one last time for **more mechanics:**

  __ typographical errors

  __ spelling errors

  __ any other small problems that were missed

  __ **Final draft** changed to single spacing

__ **Family Fiction Binder** put together, including:

  __ family interview notes

  __ family tree chart(s)

  __ historical research notes

  __ rough draft

  __ final copy of story

Instructor's Notes

Recommendations

This writing project is intended to produce a short story, the length of which should be determined by the instructor. For younger students I recommend at least three pages. Older students may choose to write up to twenty-five or more. Still others may produce a novella, which is simply a term for a work of fiction that is longer than a short story and shorter than a novel. A few may soar beyond the requirement and produce a full-length novel. So much the better!

The fact is, the more the young writer discovers about the world of his ancestors, the more his inspiration will grow. His research will leave him with more ideas for stories than he can use in one assignment. After completing this project, he need never again object by saying, with regard to historical fiction at least, "I don't know what to write about."

A writer of historical fiction has much work to do before she can sit down and actually begin writing a story. This project is designed to help the student of writing understand the process necessary to produce a work of historical fiction. It is divided into three phases:

1. Research
2. Writing
3. Editing

The research phase is vital to this assignment. The final result however, is meant to be a work of fiction. DO NOT let your student miss the point and write a factual "report" on his or her ancestor(s) that sounds like the following:

Great Grandma Bess was born in Wyoming in 1898 to Homer and Angelina Smith. She had black hair. She also had four older brothers.

Instead, the story should read as fiction:

Homer Smith smiled at his wife as he gazed at the new, black-haired baby in her arms. "Let's call her Bess," he suggested.

Angelina nodded in agreement as her four sons wrestled on the floor beside the bed.

Another temptation to avoid is trying to tell an ancestor's life story from beginning to end. Again, this assignment is not meant to be a "report." Encourage the student to choose an episode or shorter time period within her ancestor's life. It can be a one-time event that took place over a few hours, or one day, such as surviving a tornado, or killing a rattlesnake. Or it can extend over a longer period of time, such as three years served in the army during a war, a month-long voyage to another country, or a decade spent trying to survive in New York City's tenement slums. Because the final product is to be a short story, the subject's entire life is not suitable material.

Some students may be tempted to keep adding characters until there are far too many for a short story. There are no hard and fast rules on how many characters should be included, but if you, the instructor, notice that it's difficult to keep the characters straight, you will want to intervene and suggest that the student either combine several characters into one, or cut some out altogether.

Yet another temptation for the student will be to dump a truckload of historical detail into his story. Encourage the student instead to pick and choose those details that are most interesting and helpful to the plot. The student should include the details here and there in passing, so the story reads:

Henry grabbed his tin lunch bucket and hurried to the streetcar stop, as usual.

rather than:

Henry always carried his lunch in a tin bucket. People back in the 1890s traveled by streetcar in big cities, so that is how Henry traveled to work.

When your student has followed all the steps outlined in this workbook, he will have produced much more than a writing assignment. It will be a gift to the whole family, to be enjoyed for generations to come.

Optional

Before your student begins this project, you may want to recommend that he or she read one of the historical novels listed on page 3, all of which were based on each author's own family history. This will set the tone for the project and provide an example of good quality fiction writing.

Another possibility is reading one of these novels, or another historical novel of your choice, aloud to your student (if not the whole thing, then at least a chapter or two.)

Note:

The younger the student, the more you will need to be involved in each step of this curriculum: making sure she understands what to do next, helping her access the various research resources, checking whether or not the definitions she has recorded for certain words are the correct ones. Because a younger child's vocabulary is limited, you may choose to relax some of the self-editing suggestions. Look at and discuss the old photographs with the child. A child younger than the recommended age level, who in your opinion is ready to tackle this project, may require a little extra explanation and help. (Note: A very young child who has difficulty understanding the passing of time might listen to one or two memories or anecdotes shared by a grandparent, then write a two-paragraph "story" about what he has heard. This would serve as preparation for the child to take on this assignment when he is older).

Older students may need limited or no assistance. Indeed, many can dispense altogether with the dictionary and Q & A exercises if it is felt they are not needed. The important thing is that you, the instructor, are free to adapt this curriculum to whichever age group you are working with.

• All definitions are taken from Webster's Ninth New Collegiate Dictionary

Editing

The areas I have concentrated on in the editing section (overuse of adjectives, overdependence on adverbs, passive language and lack of sentence variation) are four of the most common challenges adolescent writers face. Young children are generally taught to pile on the adjectives and adverbs as a means of adding depth and color to their descriptions. This is a necessary process in their development. As they mature, however, they need to learn to pare down those dress-ups, so their writing can take on a more grown-up appearance.

Likewise, passive verbs are acceptable during the younger elementary years because the child's focus is on description rather than action. This focus must gradually shift as the student matures, emphasizing a more balanced style that keeps the story moving, thus making it more enjoyable to read. It is also tempting for a young writer to get stuck using the same subject-verb sentence formula over and over again. Varying sentence starters also contributes to readability.

Besides the obvious self-editing steps of checking for misspellings, grammar and punctuation problems, incomplete or run-on sentences, dealing effectively with the above four areas will polish the student's story significantly. The checklist on the next page will help you back up your student in the editing process. After she has completed each phase of self-editing, you can look her manuscript over for anything she missed.

Other Branches To Climb

The worksheets in this book may be photocopied and used multiple times. If desired, this writing assignment could be given once a year, or every two years, so that a student builds up a body of stories based on his ancestors.

The diligent work your student has done on this assignment will be valuable for future assignments. I didn't stop with *The Bushwhacker,* but went on to write *The Stone Grave* (*Et Sted i Hjertet,* published in Denmark by Hovedland, 2003), an adult historical novel based on a completely different set of my ancestors. Since *The Stone Grave* also takes place during the latter half of the 19th century, I was able to build upon the foundation already in place from my research for *The Bushwhacker.*

Likewise, using the interview notes, family tree charts, and historical research notes contained in the **Family Fiction Binder**, your student, when creating future works of historical fiction based on other branches of his or her family tree, will be able to build on the foundation already established through the completing of this assignment.

Answer Key

Page 2

List of things that might give an author inspiration for a story:

- A current event
- A newspaper or magazine article
- A vacation or trip to new town, state, or country
- Witnessing a funny incident
- A frightening experience
- A friend's experience
- Observing animals
- Observing people in a public place
- A brother, sister, or other family member
- Studying about a different country or culture
- Hearing a grandparent's childhood memory
- A family tradition
- A childhood memory
- A novel or biography
- A legend or folktale
- A film
- Observing an accident
- A strong belief in something
- A dream
- A fun experience
- A natural disaster
- A conversation with someone
- A story someone has told
- Celebrating a holiday
- A sad experience
- Neighborhood happenings
- A camping trip
- A happy experience

The list could go on and on. The main idea is to get the student thinking about possible sources of inspiration.

historical:

a) of, relating to, or having the character of history

b) based on history

fiction:

a) something invented by the imagination

b) an invented story

The student's definition of historical fiction should be something akin to the following:

1. An invented story that takes place in a historical setting
2. A made-up story based on history

Page 17

census: A complete enumeration (counting) of a population.

Page 15

Make Your Best Guess answers:

The purpose of this quiz is simply to demonstrate that our knowledge of historical detail is often sketchy. We may have a good idea about how things were done, but there is always more we can learn.

1. **How did farmers harvest wheat in the early 1800s?**

   The wheat was cut with cradles in the field, by the cradler. A worker called a binder followed the cradler, tying the wheat into bundles, which were stored in a barn. On threshing day, the harvested wheat was beaten with flails to separate the straw and chaff from the wheat. Winnowers used a sheet, tray or basket to toss up the wheat and catch it while the chaff and straw blew away.

2. **How did a woman on the Oregon Trail wash her family's clothing?**

   Either by scrubbing it in a river using a bar of soap, or filling a tin or wooden washtub with water heated over a fire. The laundry was scrubbed on a washboard made of metal and wood, wrung out, and laid in the sun to dry.

3. **With what would one set the table for a meal in a farmhouse in colonial America (1700s).**

   With pewter mugs, wooden trenchers (plates or bowls), pewter plates or bowls, knives and spoons made of pewter (forks were seldom used.)

4. **How did people travel from place to place during the Middle Ages in Europe?**

   Mostly by foot, along narrow dirt paths through forests. Only the rich could afford horses. Some people used light, two-wheeled carts pulled by horses. Heavy loads were transported in boats by river and sea.

Page 18

Possible sources for finding out details about the setting of a story:

- Encyclopedia
- Books about birds
- Topographical map
- Books on wildlife
- Research Tools
- Nature books
- Geography books
- Travel website
- Books containing photographs of setting

Possible sources for learning about a war and its particular battles:

- History books
- Historical film
- History expert, such as a museum docent
- Documentary
- Websites
- History teacher

Possible sources for finding out factual details about daily life (clothing, tools, housing, etc.) in a certain time period:

Encyclopedia	History books
Websites	Historical film
Old photographs	History museum
Paintings	History teacher
Video, DVD or television documentary	History expert, such as a museum docent

These resources, along with census records and facts obtained from family interviews, provide ample materials for the writer of historical fiction.

Page 19

anachronism: an error in chronology; a chronological misplacing of persons, events, objects, or customs.

chronology: the science that deals with measuring time by regular divisions and that assigns to events their proper dates

Page 20

accurate:

a) free from error

b) correct

Page 35

plot: the plan or main story of a literary work

Page 38

FACT	can be EITHER	FICTION
1. larger place names	1. smaller place names	1. dialogue
2. famous events	2. characters' names	2. characters' thoughts & feelings
3. dates of famous events	3. characters' appearance	
4. famous people	4. characters' actions	
	5. objects	

Page 45

edit:

a) to prepare for publication or public presentation

b) to alter, adapt, or refine

Instructor's Checklist

__ **(If parent)** Provided student with information to fill out the family tree chart as completely as possible

__ Checked student's interview questions to make sure they are specific and not too vague or general

__ **(If parent)** Facilitated student's interviewing of knowledgeable relatives

Facilitated student's looking at:

    __ **(If parent)** old family photographs, whether your own or another family member's

    __ general historical photographs or paintings, either in a museum, book, or on the Internet

Checked student's **Historical Research Notes** for:

    __ historical accuracy and clarity

    __ relevance to the student's planned story (i.e. don't let him spend hours researching horses if there is only brief mention of a horse in his story. Encourage him to spend time researching those things most applicable to his story)

Checked "roadmap" to be sure that:

    __ student is not trying to cover an ancestor's entire lifespan

    __ projected plot makes sense and is not too complicated for short story length

    __ (Keep in mind that the student does not have to adhere <u>strictly</u> to the roadmap and it is meant to be a rough guide.)

Checked rough draft for **"content"** (AFTER student checked it) to be sure that:

    __ the student has not missed the point and written a "report"

    __ the plot makes sense and flows well

    __ the story weaves together fact and fiction (is believable and interesting)

    __ the student has made sufficient use of historical facts and details (such as clothing, tools, chores, transportation, foods, houses, etc.)

    __ the story "rings true" historically (is historically accurate)

    __ the story contains no anachronisms

    __ there are not too many characters for the (short) story's length

    __ historical information has been "sprinkled" throughout and not "dumped"

    __ story setting is clearly established and described (place names, landscape, climate, concurrent historical events)

A NOTE TO THE INSTRUCTOR

The goal of this project is to inspire the student to take joy in writing fiction. It is our sincere hope that learning about his ancestors and the times in which they lived will foster his creativity and a passion to tell their stories. Please keep in mind that the checklist is a tool to help both you and the student make sure the story develops to its full potential. It is also a measuring stick for those wanting or needing to grade an older student. However, following the checklist to "the letter of the law" is not the main purpose of this assignment. If your student doesn't manage to accomplish to perfection everything on the checklist, yet produces the finest story he has ever written, then the project's goal has been reached and this should be reflected in his grade.

continued on next page

A NOTE TO THE INSTRUCTOR *cont.*

We encourage you, the instructor, to step back and allow the student's creativity to flow naturally. Checking his progress at certain intervals will enable you to give necessary guidance, but we caution against the kind of strong intervention that might curb the student's creativity and ownership of the project. A few well-timed reminders and suggestions should keep your student on track as he explores the world of writing historical fiction.

      __ story includes dialogue

      __ dialogue is appropriate to the story's time period and setting

Checked **first computer draft** for **STYLE** (AFTER student checked it), making sure it:

      __ has a strong title that creates interest

      __ has a strong beginning that draws the reader in

      __ does not contain too many adjectives

      __ does not contain too many adverbs

      __ does not have too much passive language

      __ contains a variety of sentence starters

      __ has a satisfying conclusion (reader is not left hanging)

      __ maintains tense throughout (not skipping back and forth between past and present tense)

Checked **second computer draft** for **MECHANICS** (AFTER student checked it):

      __ spelling errors

      __ run-on sentences

      __ incomplete sentences

      __ punctuation errors

      __ typographical errors

Checked **third computer draft** for **MORE MECHANICS** (AFTER student checked it):

      __ typographical errors

      __ spelling errors

      __ other small problems that were missed

Made sure student's **Family Fiction Binder** contains:

      ___ interview notes

      ___ family tree charts

      ___ historical research notes

      ___ rough draft

      ___ final copy of story

If desired, you can assist the younger student in making a decorative cover for the final copy of the story, perhaps including a photograph or drawing of the ancestor on whose life the story is based.

Helpful Websites

rootsweb.com

searchforancestors.com

searchforancestors.com/military.html

ancestry.com

ancestorsearch.com

census-online.com

censusfinder.com

ellisisland.org

Helpful Books

The following books are published by Writer's Digest Books, F & W Publications, Inc.

The Writer's Guide to Everyday Life in the 1800s
By Marc McCutcheon (1993)

The Writer's Guide to Everyday Life During the Civil War
By Michael J. Varhola (1999)

The Writer's Guide to Everyday Life in Renaissance England (1485-1649)
By Kathy Lynn Emerson (1996)

The Writer's Guide to Everyday Life in Colonial America
By Dale Taylor (1997)

The Writer's Guide to Everyday Life in Regency and Victorian England (1811-1901)
By Kristine Hughes (1998)

The Writer's Guide to Everyday Life Among the American Indians
By Candy Moulton (2001)

The Writer's Guide to Everyday Life in the Wild West
By Candy Moulton (1999)

The Writer's Guide to Everyday Life from Prohibition through World War II
By Marc McCutcheon

The Writer's Guide to Everyday Life in the Middle Ages
By Sherrilyn Kenyon (1995)

National Archives and Records Administration

Northeast Region:
 Boston
 380 Trapelo Rd.
 Waltham, MA 02154-6399

New York City
 201 Varick St.
 New York, NY 10014-4811

Mid-Atlantic Region:
 Center City
 Philadelphia
 900 Market St.,
 Philadelphia, PA 19107

Southeast Region:
 Headquarters
 1557 St. Joseph Ave.
 East Point, GA 30344

Great Lakes Region:
 Chicago
 7358 S. Pulaski Rd.
 Chicago, IL 60629-5898

Central Plains Region:
 Headquarters
 2312 E. Bannister Rd.
 Kansas City, MO 64131

Southwest Region:
 Headquarters
 501 W. Felix St.
 Fort Worth, TX 76115-3405

Rocky Mountain Region:
 Headquarters
 Bldg. 48, Denver Federal Ctr.
 Denver, CO 80225-0307

Pacific Region:
 Laguna Niguel
 1st. Floor E., 24000 Avila Rd.
 Laguna Niguel, CA 92677-3405

San Francisco
 1000 Commodore Dr.
 San Bruno, CA 94066

Pacific Alaska Region:
 Seattle
 6125 Sand Point Way NE.
 Seattle, WA 98115

Anchorage
 654 W. 3rd Ave., Anchorage
 AK 99501-2145

For further information, contact the Office of Regional Records Services at (301) 713-7200

Andrea's Homeschool Tips

An Introduction

During my seven years of homeschooling, I've learned to adjust curriculum based on my skill, my children's abilities, and the time allotted for our school day. Below is a plan for adapting this assignment for my children ages 13, 12, and 8. It is included to encourage other parents who may need to adapt it for their own children. While this writing project is more complex than any we have tried before, it is a worthy project to attempt and can be divided into smaller segments to make it easier to accomplish.

Writing historical fiction based on one's ancestors is an excellent idea, providing a unique opportunity to create a family treasure. A story about an ancestor is not just another creative writing assignment; it is a long-term investment, giving a glimpse into an almost forgotten past and passing it on to future generations. It is my hope that through sharing this plan for implementing the project, others with younger children will be encouraged to create this heirloom as well.

Based on the information provided in the student guide and instructor's notes, I have created suggestions for guiding 10-13 year-olds through this project and including younger children in the writing experience. These comments correspond with a suggested schedule provided in the margin. Feel free to increase or decrease the days spent on each activity depending on your children's ages and abilities, your general school day, and the length of story you feel each child is capable of writing. You know your children best, and as you go along, you will be able to determine how to adjust the schedule.

The schedule provided in the margin is designed for the parent working with a reluctant or inexperienced writer aged 10-13 who will need guidance writing a bare minimum of three pages of historical fiction. The three major parts of this project include research, writing, and editing.

Research consists of census information, the family tree, family interview, and five to ten historical facts to make the story more interesting and authentic.

The writing phase emphasizes periodic reviews of the Roadmap to help the child keep the travel plans clearly in view as the rough draft is written.

Editing focuses on the skills taught in the student guide and may be augmented with the requirements of your regular writing program.

Schedule for Younger Students

Preparation

- ☐ Read the Student Guide and Instructor's Notes
- ☐ Evaluate this schedule, making modifications
- ☐ Familiarize yourself with the recommended websites and other resources
- ☐ Prepare a Family Fiction Binder
- ☐ Copy worksheet pages for each student
- ☐ Send the family tree chart (p.6) and interview questions (p.9) to appropriate family members
- ☐ Schedule the interviews
- ☐ Start thinking about ideas for your family Presentation Night

Introduction

DAY 1
- ☐ Present the project
- ☐ Discuss the Introduction (p.1–4)

Preparation

The Family Fiction Binder

The Family Fiction Binder can be as simple as a 3-ring notebook with pockets and 5-tab dividers or as elaborate as your children's skills and imaginations can make it. Five sections will allow easy access to the information as your children work and will provide a framework for presenting the material. Any photographs or special documents can be placed in sheet protectors or kept in envelopes punched with holes to fit in the rings of the binder or simply put in the pockets. As you prepare the binder, consider what impression you want your children to leave on their descendants.

1. Final copy with illustrations
2. Family tree research including family tree charts and interview notes
3. Historical research
4. Photographs or documents
5. Drafts of the story

Family Fiction Chart and Interview Notes

Long before presenting this project to your children, you could start filling in the family chart and send the interview questions to family members so that some family research material is available when the project begins. Now would be an excellent time to start.

> **Optional Pre-project Activity**
>
> Reading *Sarah, Plain and Tall* aloud would be a wonderful way to introduce this project. It can be read within a week, even to young children, and would provide material to help discuss the writing of historical fiction. *The Courage of Sarah Noble* and *The Bears on Hemlock Mountain* by Alice Dalgliesh and *The Matchlock Gun* by Walter Edmonds are also fairly short and would work well.

Introduction

General Lesson Planning

I like planning lessons in increments of 15 or 30 minutes. Discussing the various sections of this project would probably take 30 minutes to an hour each day and could be divided into shorter sessions if necessary. I write the information on the board and ask "who," "what," "where," and "when" questions to help generate discussion and stimulate thinking.

Research

Interview

Recording the conversation on audio or videotape makes note taking easier. In a phone interview, children should at least write down the important facts of each answer. Give them time to practice beforehand. Be prepared to assist the child in the interviewing process if it turns out to be too difficult.

Historical Research

For research, I simply select two or three non-fiction books with pictures from the children's section of the library. The *Eyewitness* books are usually a good place to start. Then I look for other interesting books nearby on the shelf. *The Cornerstones of Freedom* series is a good resource for American history, packing a lot of information into a few easily read pages. We usually work together, picking out three to five interesting facts from each source, writing three key words from each fact on the board. This helps us decide which are the best five to ten facts to use for the paper.

Optional Ideas for Enhancing the Project

When we study history, I read both a non-fiction book for five to 15 minutes and a good literature book based on that time period for 15-30 minutes. *Johnny Tremain* by Esther Forbes and *Early Thunder* by Jean Fritz for the Revolutionary War, *Across Five Aprils* by Irene Hunt for the Civil War, *Island of the Blue Dolphins* by Scott O'Dell and *By the Great Horn Spoon* by Sid Fleischman for California History are examples of books that we have enjoyed. Some of our bedtime reading such as Sterling North's *Rascal,* Wilson Rawls' *Summer of the Monkeys,* and Mark Twain's *Tom Sawyer* would also provide background for American history. Children's classics, both for individual reading and reading aloud, would make good companions during the days and weeks in which the children work on their stories.

While I read, my children are free to draw, build with construction toys, or work on crafts as long as they are quiet and pay attention. This time could also be used to draw a picture or make a craft for the family tree binder or presentation night.

On Wednesdays we listen to the music of a classical composer, look at the paintings of an artist, and recite poetry. To enhance this project, try choosing a composer, artist, or a poet from the appropriate time period; or selecting a work of music, a painting, or a poem from another time or place that ties into the story.

Research

DAY 2
- ☐ Discuss the interview process (p.5,7)
- ☐ Choose your branch (p.13)

DAY 3
- ☐ Take the quiz (p.15)
- ☐ Look up census information
- ☐ Discuss resources (p.18)

DAY 4-6
- ☐ Discuss historical research (p.19–34)
- ☐ Conduct research

DAY 7
- ☐ Review research notes and interview questions
- ☐ Prepare for the interview

DAY 8
- ☐ Conduct the interview

Writing

DAY 9
- ☐ Discuss the Roadmap (p.40)
- ☐ Develop the Roadmap

DAY 10
- ☐ Refine the Roadmap

DAY 11-13
- ☐ Begin to hand write the rough draft

DAY 14
- ☐ Review the Roadmap travel plans
- ☐ Continue to hand write the rough draft

DAY 15-17
- ☐ Continue to hand write the rough draft
- ☐ Final review of the Roadmap travel plans

DAY 18
- ☐ Finish the rough draft
- ☐ Review the rough draft, checking for content

DAY 19-21
- ☐ Type the first computer draft

Writing

Suggestions for Support Resources

WriteShop and the Institute for Excellence in Writing both offer comprehensive and effective writing programs for all ages.

The plot, a simple summary of the story's events, is the basis of the Roadmap. A good resource for understanding the elements of plot as well as discussing children's literature with students of all ages is The Center for Literature's *Teaching the Classics*.

Roadmap

Because the Roadmap serves as your guide to keep your story on track, it is an essential element of this project, but it will likely be adjusted along the way, just as travel plans can change whenever you take a trip. To help prepare for the Roadmap, try creating a simple summary outline with three parts: Character & Setting, Plot & Conflict, and Climax & Resolution. We do this as a group, and I write it on the board. Though using the same outline, children will still come up with different plans for their Roadmap. Children not quite old enough to complete the writing project could simply copy the outline for an oral presentation of the story. For younger students creating their own outline, you can add an extra day to the schedule. Write the outline on the first day, the first half of the Roadmap on the second day, then finish the Roadmap on the third day.

Writing the Rough Draft

Spend 15 to 30 minutes each day writing the rough draft. Even my reluctant writers can now complete two to three paragraphs per day, especially if they are interested in the subject.

Review the Roadmap

Because this assignment relies on the intricacies of content, plot, and weaving together fact and fiction, writing check-ups based on the roadmap would be beneficial to guide the young writer's efforts every few days. These periodic check-ups would serve as a structured comparison of the roadmap and the rough draft to keep the child moving forward with his plan, or they may reveal changes that could be made to improve the roadmap and the story. Keep in mind that this is just like a travel adventure. Relax, enjoy the trip, and let your children follow their map.

Each day, however, a more informal review of the day's writing could be accomplished simply by reading aloud what has been written. We do this with our regular writing projects, and it usually helps uncover changes that could or should be made. It also helps the children get over the fear of having their creative work read aloud. Sometimes I read it, sometimes they do, but it is an easy way to help them develop their writing skills without a lot of input from me.

Typing The First Computer Draft

The typing ability of 10-13 year olds varies greatly. Give your children enough time each day to comfortably type their first draft. Type it yourself if they have little or no typing skills, but have them sit with you to dictate any changes.

Editing

Additional Resources

Whenever I encounter difficult writing questions I cannot answer off the top of my head, I turn to *The Elements of Style,* fondly referred to as "Strunk and White." Co-author E.B. White wrote *Charlotte's Web.*

Ideas for Building Style

We first became acquainted with stylistic techniques through adverbs. I asked my children to think of some "ly" words. To help them become more familiar with these adverbs, I paused and repeated them when we came across them in our reading or discussions. Because that was so effective, I continue to emphasize the new techniques we are learning in that same manner.

Although we keep a thesaurus, a dictionary, and lists of words handy whenever we work on writing, we have often had difficulty discovering strong verbs since the thesaurus generally just provides synonyms. The verbs we find in the thesaurus are somewhat stronger, but still don't always capture the specific action we are trying to describe. Sometimes I try acting out the movement to help us identify a better choice for a weak verb.

Presentation

After completing their writing projects, my children read them aloud, usually after dinner, so that my husband can hear what they have written. I remind them to count to three (silently) before they begin and after they finish. This is a simple way of acknowledging the work they have completed.

The scope of this project, however, lends itself to a special night of celebration. In the homeschooling community, we do not have a natural setting for show and tell beyond our immediate family. We have to create those opportunities. Extended family could be invited to a presentation night to hear the family tree stories. Groups of families working separately on this project could get together for dinner or dessert and share one another's stories. Your children might have an opportunity to read their stories in a more informal gathering of one or two other families in which the children present their various creations or talents. You could take pictures or act out the stories and videotape the performance. The important thing is to emphasize the achievement so that it will have a more lasting impact.

Editing

DAY 22
☐ Discuss editing (p.45-49)

DAY 23-26
☐ Edit the first computer draft checking for style

☐ Edit the second and third computer drafts checking for mechanics

☐ Complete the Final

Preservation

☐ Complete the Family Fiction Binder

Presentation

☐ Celebrate with a Presentation Night

Grading Guide

Content – 34 Points Possible

Story reads as fiction and not as a "report"	14
Plot makes sense and flows well	2
Story weaves together fact and fiction (is believable and interesting)	2
Story contains enough historical facts to make the reader feel like he or she is "in" the time period and setting (for example: descriptions of clothing, food, travel, tools, chores, houses, etc.)	2
Story is historically accurate	2
Story contains no anachronisms	2
Story (short) doesn't have too many characters	2
Historical facts are "sprinkled throughout the story and not "dumped"	2
Story's setting is clearly described (place names, landscape, climate, true historical events)	2
Story includes dialogue	2
Dialogue is appropriate to the story's time period and setting	2
	TOTAL POINTS

Style – 22 Points

Story has a strong title that creates interest	4
Story has a strong beginning that draws the reader in	4
Story does not have too many adjectives	2
Story contains strong verbs and not too many adverbs	2
Story does not have too much passive language	2
Story has a good variety of sentence starters	2
Story has a satisfying conclusion (reader is not left hanging)	4
Tense is consistent (the story doesn't jump back and forth between past and present tense)	2
	TOTAL

Mechanics – 14 Points

Correct spelling	2	_____
Run-on sentences eliminated	2	_____
Incomplete sentences eliminated	2	_____
Correct punctuation	2	_____
Correct typing	2	_____
Other small problems effectively dealt with	2	_____
Single spacing	2	_____
	TOTAL	_____

Family Fiction Binder – 10 Points

Family interview notes	2	_____
Family tree chart(s)	2	_____
Historical research notes	2	_____
Rough draft	2	_____
Final copy of story	2	_____

Individual Writing Program – 20 Points   20   _____

TOTAL   _____

100 Points Possible

Family Tree

Family Tree